For Holly, Karen, Ann, Karina, and Yvetta

First edition 2007

Library of Congress Cataloging-in-Publication Data is available.

Library of Congress Catalog Card Number 2006046288

ISBN 978-0-7636-2919-9

2 4 6 8 10 9 7 5 3 1

Printed in Singapore

This book was typeset in Alghera.
The illustrations were done in ink and watercolor,
with digitally colorized backgrounds.

Candlewick Press
2067 Massachusetts Avenue
Cambridge, Massachusetts 02140

visit us at www.candlewick.com

Taking a Bath with the Dog
and Other Things that Make Me Happy

SCOTT MENCHIN

CANDLEWICK PRESS
CAMBRIDGE, MASSACHUSETTS

I miss
your smile
today,
Sweet Pea.
What would
make you
happy?

I don't know.

What makes you happy?

Taking a bath!

What makes you happy?

Counting.

What makes you happy?

What makes you happy?

Shoes.

What makes you happy?

Playing with my hair.

What makes you happy?

Digging.

What makes you happy?

Stripes.

What makes you happy?

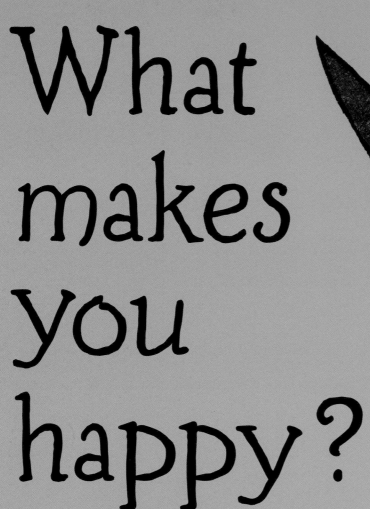

Sleeping
upside down.

What
makes
you
happy?

Smiling.

Hmmmm . . .

Sweet Pea, you're smiling. Did you find out what makes you happy?

Yes!

I'm happy when I . . .

Tickle my baby brother.  Jump rope.

 Bake cookies with faces.  Ride my bike.

Chew peas one at a time.  Make a wish.

 Stay up late.  Paint on eggs.

Make faces.  Hold my breath underwater.

 Stick finger puppets on my toes.  Sing.

Slurp spaghetti.  Look at my reflection.

 Dance with my shadow.  Play dress-up.

Sit in my dad's chair.  Blow bubbles.

 Drink tea with Grandma.  Play drums.

Pretend I'm a monster.  Swim at night.

 Lick sprinkles off ice cream. And . . .

I'm happy when I'm taking a bath with the dog!

Mom, you're smiling.
You must be happy too!